CHRIS VAN ALLSBURG

JUST A DREAM

sandpiper

Houghton Mifflin Harcourt
Boston New York

"We have met the enemy and he is us."

—Pogo

The Library of Congress has cataloged the hardcover edition as follows:
Van Allsburg, Chris.
Just a dream / Chris Van Allsburg.
p. cm.
Summary: When he has a dream about a future Earth devastated by pollution,
Walter begins to understand the importance of taking care of the environment.

ISBN: 978-0-395-53308-6 hardcover
ISBN: 978-0-547-52026-1 paperback

Manufactured in Singapore
TWP 10 9 8 7 6 5 4 3 2 1

4500269643

JUST A DREAM

As usual, Walter stopped at the bakery on his way home from school. He bought one large jelly-filled doughnut. He took the pastry from its bag, eating quickly as he walked along. He licked the red jelly from his fingers. Then he crumpled up the empty bag and threw it at a fire hydrant.

At home Walter saw Rose, the little girl next door, watering a tree that had just been planted. "It's my birthday present," she said proudly. Walter couldn't understand why anyone would want a tree for a present. His own birthday was just a few days away, "And I'm not getting some dumb plant," he told Rose.

After dinner Walter took out the trash. Three cans stood next to the garage. One was for bottles, one for cans, and one for everything else. As usual, Walter dumped everything into one can. He was too busy to sort through garbage, especially when there was something good on television.

The show that Walter was so eager to watch was about a boy who lived in the future. The boy flew around in a tiny airplane that he parked on the roof of his house. He had a robot and a small machine that could make any kind of food with the push of a button.

Walter went to bed wishing he lived in the future. He couldn't wait to have his own tiny plane, a robot to take out the trash, and a machine that could make jelly doughnuts by the thousands. When he fell asleep, his wish came true. That night Walter's bed traveled to . . .

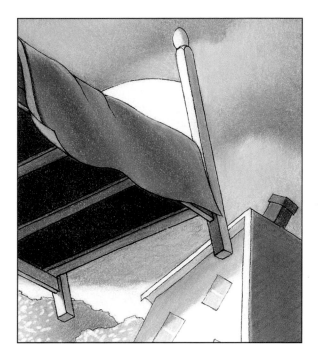

the future.

Walter woke up in the middle of a huge dump. A bulldozer was pushing a heap of bulging trash bags toward him. "Stop!" he yelled.

The man driving the bulldozer put his machine in neutral. "Oh, sorry," he said. "Didn't see you."

Walter looked at the distant mountains of trash and saw half-buried houses. "Do people live here?" he asked.

"Not anymore," answered the man.

A few feet from the bed was a rusty old street sign that read FLORAL AVENUE. "Oh no," gasped Walter. He lived on Floral Avenue.

The driver revved up his bulldozer. "Well," he shouted, "back to work!"

Walter pulled the covers over his head. This can't be the future, he thought. I'm sure it's just a dream. He went back to sleep.

But not for long . . .

Walter peered over the edge of his bed, which was caught in the branches of a tall tree. Down below, he could see two men carrying a large saw. "Hello!" Walter yelled out.

"Hello to you!" they shouted back.

"You aren't going to cut down this tree, are you?" Walter asked.

But the woodcutters didn't answer. They took off their jackets, rolled up their sleeves, and got to work. Back and forth they pushed the saw, slicing through the trunk of Walter's tree. "You must need this tree for something important," Walter called down.

"Oh yes," they said, "very important." Then Walter noticed lettering on the woodcutters' jackets. He could just make out the words: QUALITY TOOTHPICK COMPANY. Walter sighed and slid back under the blankets.

Until . . .

Walter couldn't stop coughing. His bed was balanced on the rim of a giant smokestack. The air was filled with smoke that burned his throat and made his eyes itch. All around him, dozens of smokestacks belched thick clouds of hot, foul smoke. A workman climbed one of the stacks.

"What is this place?" Walter called out.

"This is the Maximum Strength Medicine Factory," the man answered.

"Gosh," said Walter, looking at all the smoke, "what kind of medicine do they make here?"

"Wonderful medicine," the workman replied, "for burning throats and itchy eyes."

Walter started coughing again.

"I can get you some," the man offered.

"No thanks," said Walter. He buried his head in his pillow and, when his coughing stopped, fell asleep.

But then . . .

Snowflakes fell on Walter. He was high in the mountains. A group of people wearing snowshoes and long fur coats hiked past his bed.

"Where are you going?" Walter asked.

"To the hotel," one of them replied.

Walter turned around and saw an enormous building. A sign on it read HOTEL EVEREST. "Is that hotel," asked Walter, "on the top of Mount Everest?"

"Yes," said one of the hikers. "Isn't it beautiful?"

"Well," Walter began. But the group didn't wait for his answer. They waved goodbye and marched away. Walter stared at the flashing yellow sign, then crawled back beneath his sheets.

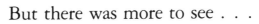

But there was more to see . . .

Walter's hand was wet and cold. When he opened his eyes, he found himself floating on the open sea, drifting toward a fishing boat. The men on the boat were laughing and dancing.

"Ship ahoy!" Walter shouted.

The fishermen waved to him.

"What's the celebration for?" he asked.

"We've just caught a fish," one of them yelled back. "Our second one this week!" They held up their small fish for Walter to see.

"Aren't you supposed to throw the little ones back?" Walter asked.

But the fishermen didn't hear him. They were busy singing and dancing.

Walter turned away. Soon the rocking of the bed put him to sleep.

But only for a moment . . .

A loud, shrieking horn nearly lifted Walter off his mattress. He jumped up. There were cars and trucks all around him, horns honking loudly, creeping along inch by inch. Every driver had a car phone in one hand and a big cup of coffee in the other. When the traffic stopped completely, the honking grew even louder. Walter could not get back to sleep.

Hours passed, and he wondered if he'd be stuck on this highway forever. He pulled his pillow tightly around his head. This can't be the future, he thought. Where are the tiny airplanes, the robots? The honking continued into the night, until finally, one by one, the cars became quiet as their drivers, and Walter, went to sleep.

But his bed traveled on . . .

Walter looked up. A horse stood right over his bed, staring directly at him. In the saddle was a woman wearing cowboy clothes. "My horse likes you," she said.

"Good," replied Walter, who wondered where he'd ended up this time. All he could see was a dull yellow haze.

"Son," the woman told him, spreading her arms in front of her, "this is the mighty Grand Canyon."

Walter gazed into the foggy distance.

"Of course," she went on, "with all this smog, nobody's gotten a good look at it for years." The woman offered to sell Walter some postcards that showed the canyon in the old days. "They're real pretty," she said.

But he couldn't look. It's just a dream, he told himself. I know I'll wake up soon, back in my room.

But he didn't . . .

Walter looked out from under his sheets. His bed was flying through the night sky. A flock of ducks passed overhead. One of them landed on the bed, and to Walter's surprise, he began to speak. "I hope you don't mind," the bird said, "if I take a short rest here." The ducks had been flying for days, looking for the pond where they had always stopped to eat.

"I'm sure it's down there somewhere," Walter said, though he suspected something awful might have happened. After a while the duck waddled to the edge of the bed, took a deep breath, and flew off. "Good luck," Walter called to him. Then he pulled the blanket over his head. "It's just a dream," he whispered, and wondered if it would ever end.

Then finally . . .

Walter's bed returned to the present. He was safe in his room again, but
he felt terrible. The future he'd seen was not what he'd expected. Robots
and little airplanes didn't seem very important now. He looked out his
window at the trees and lawns in the early morning light, then jumped
out of bed.

He ran outside and down the block, still in his pajamas. He found the empty jelly doughnut bag he'd thrown at the fire hydrant the day before. Then Walter went back home and, before the sun came up, sorted all the trash by the garage.

A few days later, on Walter's birthday, all his friends came over for cake and ice cream. They loved his new toys: the laser gun set, electric yo-yo, and inflatable dinosaurs. "My best present," Walter told them, "is outside." Then he showed them the gift that he'd picked out that morning — a tree.

After the party, Walter and his dad planted the birthday present. When he went to bed, Walter looked out his window. He could see his tree and the tree Rose had planted on her birthday. He liked the way they looked, side by side. Then he went to sleep, but not for long, because that night Walter's bed took him away again.

When Walter woke up, his bed was standing in the shade of two tall trees. The sky was blue. Laundry hanging from a clothesline flapped in the breeze. A man pushed an old motorless lawn mower. This isn't the future, Walter thought. It's the past.

"Good morning," the man said. "You've found a nice place to sleep."

"Yes, I have," Walter agreed. There was something very peaceful about the huge trees next to his bed.

The man looked up at the rustling leaves. "My great-grandmother planted one of these trees," he said, "when she was a little girl."

Walter looked up at the leaves too, and realized where his bed had taken him. This was the future, after all, a different kind of future. There were still no robots or tiny airplanes. There weren't even any clothes dryers or gas-powered lawn mowers. Walter lay back and smiled. "I like it here," he told the man, then drifted off to sleep in the shade of the two giant trees — the trees he and Rose had planted so many years ago.